For Georgia, the star that never fails to shine

Prologue

There was a sparkle of snowflakes on Christmas Eve. Badger the Mystical Mutt had just received his first Christmas parcel. He eyed the colourful round package eagerly and poked it gently. A higgledy-piggledy tower of freshly buttered toast sat untouched beside him.

It could be a ball, or maybe it's a pile of circular toast, he thought, scratching his head and taking a bite from the tower of toast. He lifted it up, shook it, held it to his ear, then spun it around and gave it some serious sniffing. *Do I really have to wait until Christmas Day before I can find out what it is?* He sighed, munching on another slice of toast. Then he spotted the gift tag. It was from his relative in the Ring of Brodgar, Captain Bravebark, with strict instructions to be opened immediately. *Toastastic*! grinned Badger as he set upon the wrapping paper and ripped it off. Inside, he found a beautiful shiny snow globe and a glittery envelope.

Badger set the snow globe down carefully next to his toast and opened the envelope nervously. Whenever he'd received a letter from Captain Bravebark before, it meant he had to do something or go somewhere. He was just getting into Christmas mode, looking forward to many feasts over the festive season and putting his paws up for a while.

He read the verse aloud:

"*Merry Christmas, Badger.*
I bring you news of woe.
Christmas is in danger
From clouds that hang so low.

The Snow Goose has a mission
To deliver the brightest star
Into its prime position,
To shine its light out far.

There's a plot to steal her prize
And fill the world with gloom.
We need a minder in the skies,
To protect us from this doom.

Shake the magic snow globe
Then you will clearly see
Exactly what the problem is
... And where you need to be.

But make it quick and snappy
It's Christmas Eve today

To make this Christmas happy
You must act without delay

Badger gulped and shook the snow globe hard.

Chapter One

Badger peered into the snow globe. His eyes widened in horror as a dreary image emerged –the much-feared Foggies, the dark, heavy thunderclouds and well-known Dumpers of Gloom. He recognised some of the clouds individually. There was Numdrum, the notorious Director of Doom, leading the annual Cloud Summit in the dingy Mopery, and his two dastardly deputies, Humdrum and Dumdrum, also known in certain cloud circles as the "Bleak Brothers", were breezing and blustering nearby. Badger leaned in further and his ears twitched. He could just about make out the sinister mumblings.

"This is our only chance to snatch the North Star and wipe out light forever," rasped Numdrum. "It's been for its

1,000-year *resparkle* at the Spangle Spa and is due to return to its usual place at the North Pole in time for Christmas."

"But surely it's protected by the Northern Lights force field?" piped up a voice from the murky recess of the summit; a voice that was very well known to Badger.

Surely that can't be my old cloud chum, Nippy Nimbus? thought Badger. *He's cranky and crabbit, but I wouldn't have thought he'd be involved with this ghastly gathering.*

He listened even closer.

"The force field only serves as protection when the North Star is actually at the North Pole where Santa Paws lives. Currently it's somewhere in Greenland with a snow goose as its guardian, and it's our job to find out where. Then we can kidnap it on its journey," Numdrum wheezed in reply.

"So, you need to stop the snow goose in mid-flight and seize the star? I understand the plan, but I don't see *why* you are so keen to extinguish the joy and jingle of Christmas forever," said a familiar voice from the back.

"Because every Christmas the Big and Wee Folk blame us if the weather isn't frosty or snowy. They call us the *Sparkle Bandits* if we dare to be wet and gloomy. We're fed up! It's time to revolt. We will plunge the world into darkness. Any trace of light and joy will disappear. Heh heh!" sniggered Numdrum. "If the North Star is not at the North Pole in time, then Christmas can't happen and tomorrow will be a complete blackout."

Badger sat back, frowned and took another bite of toast. He was shocked that Nippy Nimbus could be part of a plot to steal the famous star from the sky. He was even more stunned at the Sparkle Bandits' spiteful plan to stop Christmas from happening.

Suddenly the snow globe began to flicker from dark to light. Badger shook it vigorously and stared at the settling image. He could see a brilliant white creature with massive wings, a beak and a grin. It was star-jumping, reverse-kicking and honking loudly, all at the same time. Strangely, it was wearing a pair of bright pink welly boots.

Is this the Snow Goose, the Guardian of the North Star and Numdrum's target? wondered Badger. His ears twitched again and he leaned in to decipher the honking hullabaloo.

"Wing-span expansion exercises completed. Inbuilt navigation rebooted, although the reverse-kicking was a bit ouch!" flapped the snow goose looking down at the welly boots. "Now I just need to apply my sleek-beak salve and I'm good to go."

This is definitely the snow goose getting ready for a big trip, Badger chuckled. He reached for his last piece of toast and reread the rhyme in Captain Bravebark's letter.

There's a plot to steal her prize
And fill the world with gloom.
We need a minder in the skies,
To protect us from this doom.

He looked fondly at his trusty flying machine, the Wim-Wim for a wowser to wind the weather up on a wet day. It was festooned with festive tinsel.

"It looks like Captain Bravebark has given us a very serious mission. Are you ready?" he asked.

The Wim-Wim whirred and hummed, clanked and clunked and shoogled its chassis. It was delighted with its latest modification, which was an early Christmas present from Badger – a super-duper pair of skis; just the job for any snowy escapades.

Badger packed some more toast and climbed aboard the Wim-Wim. He placed the snow globe on the dashboard and set the navigation system for due north.

But at the very same time as Badger set off, over at the Mopery, another emergency Cloud Summit was taking place and the atmosphere was dark ... extremely dark.

Chapter Two

The Wim-Wim cruised through the crisp, cold, clear northern sky. Its tinsel sparkled brightly reflecting the twinkling stars.

As Badger pulled his neckerchief closer for warmth, he was startled by a loud rumble.

"Oops, pardon me," he said to no one in particular, realising it was his own tummy. "It must be time for a snack." He took out a slice of toast from his secret stash. He was mid-crunch when a wisp of green light swirled around him. Badger looked out to see the sky ablaze with colour. Heavenly lights of streaming hues of blue, purple and red were draped like curtains in front of him, and swooshed across the sky. He watched in awe and smiled.

It was the Aurora Borealis – the Northern Lights – welcoming him to the southern tip of Greenland with a multicoloured extravaganza.

"Amazing! It's like a dancing horizontal rainbow," he said to the Wim-Wim. "What a beautiful sight!"

The Wim-Wim purred in agreement as Badger pulled the throttle and prepared for landing. The flying machine dipped downwards for the final descent through the Northern Lights.

"Over there!" shouted the Mystical Mutt as he spotted a bright white glow through the changing colours. It appeared to be on top of a lone Christmas tree, in the middle of nowhere, in Greenland.

"Greenland doesn't look very green to me, apart from that tree," he muttered, looking at the snow-covered land.

"It was a brilliant idea to fit those skis," he smiled smugly, as the Wim-Wim landed softly and slid neatly to a stop.

Badger climbed down the Wim-Wim's ladder. He sniffed the fresh cold air and looked around at the "not so green" Greenland. All he could hear was the crunch of snow under his paws as he headed towards the vivid lights of the tree.

Suddenly, he heard a loud HONK! HONK! HONK! A big thrashing, flapping bird flew straight at him and knocked him flat into the snow.

"Ouch!" yelled Badger. He looked up to see a huge beak looking down at him curiously.

"I'm terribly sorry," said the bird, "but who *are* you, and what *is* that contraption?"

"Erm, I'm Badger the Mystical Mutt and you appear to have landed on my head," winced Badger. "And *that* is my Wim-Wim."

"Wim-what?" asked the large bird.

"Wim-Wim: my travelling machine.
And you're still on my head. I can't move,"
whimpered Badger, his nose numbing with
the cold.

"You're definitely Badger the Mystical
Mutt?" replied the big beak. "*The* Badger
the Mystical the Mystical Mutt? The legend
that is the world's most magical dog? Mind
you, I've heard your magic is a bit hit or
miss ..."

"Yes!" cried Badger. "I am! But I'll be
Badger the *Frozen* Mutt if you don't get off
my head. This snow is really cold and if you
are who I think *you* are, then I really need to
talk to you. Now!"

"Sorry," said the bird as it shuffled onto
the snow to face him. "I had to be sure."

With pink wellies, a white downy body
and a great big grin, it was definitely the
snow goose he'd seen in his snow globe. She
tilted her head, flapped her massive wings
and said, "I'm Gabriella, but you can call me
Ella."

Badger stood up and shook himself.

"Ella, I am very pleased to meet you. I believe you have been chosen to take the North Star safely to its rightful place in the sky in time to shine its light around the world for Christmas."

"I have indeed" said Ella, puffing out her chest proudly.

"Then I am here to help you. I have been sent to warn you of a dastardly plan." Badger grimaced. "It's those Sparkle Bandits, the Foggies. They're plotting to follow you and steal the star. Their hope for a world of darkness is very strong. They know the Guardian of the Star is a Snow Goose, and you, Ella, are most definitely a snow goose."

"I know, it's a dangerous mission," said Ella. "I'm a step ahead already, look!" She pointed over to the one and only Christmas tree and its dazzling star.

"Where did you get that tree?" asked Badger, wondering how a tree could help them. "It's very ... *unusual.*"

"I made it," said Ella proudly. "It's amazing what you can do with some sticks, rocks and a bit of creeping juniper."

"That's, well ... *interesting*," said Badger, looking at the slightly wonky, tilting and wilting Christmas tree with its star on top. "But what has it got to do with our task?"

"It's *the* star," she whispered. "The North Star."

The Mystical Mutt smiled. "Aha, Ella! Very clever. You're hiding it in plain sight. But the Foggies, led by Numdrum and the Bleak Brothers, see this as their chance to ruin everything. Will you let me help you?" asked Badger hopefully.

"Wow, yes! I'd love some company, especially that of a celebrity dog," said Ella excitedly.

"Then, as today is Christmas Eve, we must go now and we must travel in the Wim-Wim. If the Foggies see you flying alone then we're scuppered. Firstly, we need to disguise this star for transit. We can't take a Christmas tree with us."

"But how can you disguise a star?" said Ella, a little peeved that they couldn't take the tree.

"With my ancient *Razzle-Dazzle* spell of course" said Badger with a swagger. "Keep very still and watch this."

Badger closed his eyes. Sparkles of light appeared around him as he addressed the star respectfully.

"Star of wonder, star of night,
Scatter your beams to strings of light.
Razzle your dazzle and smuggle your glory
With sparkles and spangles to safe-keep
your story."

Badger looked at Ella. Ella shuffled and
looked at Badger. They both looked at the
star and waited.

The tree started to wobble,
then the star began to
shudder and shot upwards
at supersonic speed. It
whirled around and then
burst into a multitude of
fairy lights. The twinkles
whooshed towards them
and wrapped
them both up
swiftly like
a glittering
Christmas
present.
"Woooaaahhhh!

Not quite as I had planned!" yelled Badger. Ella honked with laughter and said: "Is this why your magic is hit or miss?"

"Very funny, Ella. Come on, we need to decorate the Wim-Wim. It's time to add some lights to the tinsel," beamed Badger.

"They'll never know it's the star," gasped Ella.

"It's genius," said Badger, "even though I say so myself."

They shoogled and shook themselves free of the lights. Then Ella took them in her beak and soared to the top of the Wim-Wim, flying loop the loop as she placed the lengthy string of fairy lights perfectly in position.

Badger bumbled about the Wim-Wim making sure he had enough supplies for them both.

"That's toast, more toast, secret stash of toast, water, snow globe, blankets, grasses and grains for Ella's dinner … and a bit more toast. Marvellous!" he muttered to himself.

"That's a *lot* of toast," said Ella.

You can never have too much toast," said Badger gravely. "Let's go!"

The Wim-Wim clanked and clunked before whizzing up from the sparkling snow into the star-filled sky.

Back at the Mopery, the Sparkle Bandits were gathering to make the very same journey.

"If that star is going to be in place for Christmas Day, then it must be on its way by now," boomed Numdrum to the assembled strata. "Thunder clouds, get ready to rumble!"

The thunder clouds shifted and skulked in the damp depths of the airless Mopery. They jostled into position.

Numdrum glanced back to give his deputies the nod, but they weren't there.

There was a kerfuffle going on somewhere in the convoy. In the scramble to be first behind their leader, the Bleak Brothers bumped and grumbled at each other. All of the other clouds floated past them silently. Numdrum groaned. His deputies were at the back, arguing.

"I'm first," declared Dumdrum.

"No, *I'm* first," claimed Humdrum.

"I think you'll find it's *my* turn," insisted Dumdrum.

"Not!"

"Is ..."

"Silence!" ordered Numdrum.

The Bleak Brothers stopped and looked around, realising they had fallen behind the others.

"Er, sorry," said Humdrum nervously.

Numdrum bristled, swept along the convoy, hauled them to the front and bashed their billows together.

"Right, don't say another word! We'll be late. Just follow me."

"Sorry," whispered Dumdrum.

Numdrum sighed, and then he boomed "Thunderclouds ... three, two, one, go!"

With a roar and a rumble they were off and on their way to stop Christmas.

Chapter Three

"I feel like I'm inside a flying Christmas tree," chuckled Badger, surrounded by the tinsel and lights of the Wim-Wim.

"All we need is a star to place on top," he winked.

Ella beamed with delight. "See, we should have brought my wonky tree after all."

"Sorry, it was too big for the Wim-Wim, Ella," smiled Badger.

It must be nearly Christmas because it's started to snow!" said Ella, snapping at snowflakes with her beak.

The Wim-Wim shone as Badger sounded the hooter, pulled the blankets around them and began to sing. Ella joined in with her honky-tonk tones as "We wish you a merry Christmas, we wish you a merry Christmas" rang out across the sky.

As the cloud convoy drifted on, Numdrum suddenly stopped. The Bleak Brothers bumped into him when he shouted "Halt!" His huge brows furrowed. "Listen, can you hear that?"

"Hear what?" asked Humdrum.

"That ... *singing* sound," the Director of Doom hissed.

The Bleak Brothers shook themselves and listened hard as tinkly tunes of Christmas cheer floated through the sky.

"*We wish you ...*" came the song.

"*... a merry Christmas,*" chorused the Bleak Brothers. Numdrum whirled around, clouted them together and sighed.

"Sorry." They both shrugged.

Numdrum flurried and muttered under his breath, "Unbelievable!" He peered into the night at a distant sparkle and familiar shape.

"Well, well, well. I do believe it's Badger the Mystical Mutt and his pesky flying machine. And if I'm not mistaken, that is the honking sound of a snow goose. I think we've located our star."

He puffed himself up and yelled, "Thunderclouds, forward! Prepare to storm!"

Back in the Wim-Wim, Badger and Ella snuggled up as a freezing current of wind gusted up from behind. The Wim-Wim bumped. They jumped.

"Woaahhh! It's just a bit of turbulence," assured the Mystical Mutt settling down again. "It's nothing to worry about. My Wim-Wim can handle this."

29

Then they felt another bump, and a bang, and a bash as the wind got stronger. Suddenly, torrents of hailstones battered against the Wim-Wim's bodywork.

Thud! Whack! Smash! The Wim-Wim shook as the turbulence pounded. The gusts of wind got stronger and the hailstones hammered harder. Badger frantically twiddled the dials on the navigation system and shouted, "At this rate, we'll be blown way off course. We'll never make it to the North Pole in time for Christmas.

He looked out in fear. Dark clouds circled them as more bumps and knocks jolted the Wim-Wim.

"Ella, push the Weather-Warning switch to *Thunder Rumble*, and turn the key up a notch. I'll tune the *Oomph* dial and make sure the propeller whizzer is still in position," he cried over the blast of the wind.

The Wim-Wim churned. Badger and Ella held on. The blizzard blew in hard and fast. The wind whistled and roared around them

as the dark clouds drew closer. Visibility was getting extremely low.

"It's a good job we've got these extra lights," yelled Badger, "or we wouldn't be able to see a thing."

The clouds battered the poor Wim-Wim with their spectacular storm. The navigation needles whirred wildly in all directions. The time-travelling machine's weather vane spun out of control. The Wim-Wim whooshed up, rolled around, then plunged downwards as the clouds took gleeful turns to bat it back and forward like a ping-pong ball.

"It's the Foggies. They've found us," yelled Badger over the deafening downpour. He looked anxiously from side to side.

"Clouds to the left of me, floaters to the right ..."

"And I'm stuck in the middle with you," screeched Ella to Badger.

He frowned and shouted, "Hold on tight."

Two huge gloomy clouds gusted determinedly towards the Wim-Wim. They rumbled and rasped: "Twinkle twinkle little star, you won't get so very far." It was the Bleak Brothers, sniggering and feeling bold.

The clouds weaved around them, whizzing and spinning into a mighty tornado. The Wim-Wim was helpless. It spiralled down and down, then spun even further downwards at breakneck speed.

"Can't you do a spell?" yelled Ella. "Too late!" Badger looked out and saw the ground below rush towards him. "Mountain!" he yelled. "Brace yourself. It's going to be a bumpy landing!"

Whump! The Wim-Wim crashed into the deep snow. Badger and Ella were catapulted out into a tangle of tinsel. All was eerily quiet. Badger couldn't move. "Er, I think you might be on top of my head again," he said, looking up to see two pink welly boots sticking out of his eyebrows.

"Sorry," said Ella, falling onto the snow beside him. "Badger?" said Ella, feeling a bit dizzy. "Do you see what I see?"

They both looked around uneasily. Dark, ominous clouds, as big as a herd of elephants, surrounded them, with Numdrum and the Bleak Brothers in front. The clouds wafted closer. The air was strangely still.

In the distance, Badger thought he could see Nippy Nimbus again, lurking shiftily.

"Right!" commanded Numdrum, "before we search the Goose for the star we know you have, what are *you* – the Mystical Mutt – doing *here*?"

Badger scanned the clouds behind Numdrum hoping to catch sight again of Nippy Nimbus who, he was sure, would vouch for him. But his one-time friend remained silent and edged out of view.

"Er ... I was going on holiday with my friend Ella," fibbed Badger. Out of the side of his eye, he thought he could see Captain Bravebark's snow globe buried upside down in the tinsel tangle.

All of a sudden Ella started humming, "Catch a falling star, Put it in your pocket, Never let it fade away."

Badger looked at her anxiously and mouthed, "What are you doing?"

"We don't have time for games. Bleak Brothers – search them until you find the star," ordered Numdrum.

"So, erm, empty your pockets," said Humdrum in his most commanding tone. He was more than a little star-struck at meeting Badger.

"Dogs don't have pockets and neither do geese," barked Badger.

"Under your hat then," said Dumdrum in his most powerful puff.

"I'm not wearing a hat, and neither is Ella. Next?"

"Up your sleeves then?" they both asked hopefully.

"I don't have any sleeves."

"What about that fancy neckerchief? What's under that?" Humdrum and Dumdrum blew on 'Chief until it billowed upwards to cover Badger's face.

"No, nothing there either," said Badger.

The Bleak Brothers looked to their master, Numdrum.

"Uh, what now, boss?"

"Seize that flying contraption, of course, you pair of numpties. They must have hidden it inside," spewed Numdrum.

"You'll never find it," honked Ella defiantly.

"Oh, but we totally will," warned the Director of Doom. "And you will forever be remembered as the most unreliable snow goose ever – the Goose who stopped Christmas."

Ella scowled.

The clouds retreated with the Wim-Wim in their midst and left Badger and Ella on top of the mountain.

"I'd packed extra toast in the Wim-Wim," said Badger wistfully.

Ella looked at him incredulously. "This is not the time to be thinking about your tummy, Badger. They've got the North Star!"

"Yes, but they don't know they have ... yet."

"What do you mean, they don't know *yet*?"

"Erm," admitted Badger, "I might have made a small error, because when I did the spell, I had to think of a *change-back* time, so that when we reached the North Pole, the star would reform to hang in its pole position, as itself, not as a bunch of fairy lights. Unfortunately, I didn't factor in whirlwinds and searches and interrogations, so the North Star will be shining again in its full dazzling glory very soon."

"Oh, no, what are we going to do? We don't even know where they've gone."

"Ah," said Badger, "but I know somebody who might know. I spotted an old friend of mine earlier, at the back of the Foggies. Let's go and see Nippy Nimbus"

"You have a friend among the baddies?" Ella eyed him suspiciously.

"Well, I hope so."

"How can we go and see him without the Wim-Wim? I can fly, but dogs can't."

"This one can. Follow me," he grinned. "And let's just take this with us too." Badger picked up the snow globe from the tinsel and dusted off the snowflakes.

At the Mopery, the clouds gathered around the Wim-Wim trying to figure out where the North Star could be hidden. But little did they know it was right in front of them, draped around the outside as fairy lights. They peered intently at the time-travelling machine. Suddenly they heard a loud *pop!* Then another *pop!* They stared at the Wim-Wim as the fairy lights slowly began to unravel from the bodywork. With each *pop!* a shimmer of light fizzed like a sparkler. Then all of the sparklers began to swirl around and around like a Catherine wheel, getting bigger, faster and faster, whizzing and fizzing, whooping and whistling. Then they exploded into one brilliant light.

Numdrum sneered, "Well, well, well. What do we have here then? Our very own star ... a soon-to-be *invisible* star."

Chapter Four

"Wow," grinned Ella, "You might not have wings like me, but I'm impressed with your propeller tail and paw action."

Badger smiled proudly as they flew side by side towards his grumpy friend, Nippy Nimbus. "Veer left, Ella. I can see him over there," yelled Badger.

Ella and Badger swooped sharply and flapped to a stop in mid-air above Nippy before landing gently in the fluff. Nippy groaned.

"I thought it wouldn't be long before you turned up. You're like a bad smell, Badger."

"Where are all your pals, Nippy?" asked Badger.

"What do you mean?" huffed the cloud.

"I saw you with the Sparkle Bandits, when they took my Wim-Wim. You were there, and you let them take it. I thought you were my friend."

"I *am* your friend, Badger, even though you irritate me hugely."

"So why are you friends with the Foggies? They're baddies," asked Badger.

Nippy sighed. "Now listen carefully, Badger. I'm working under cover. I have to pretend to be part of the plot so that I can find out what the Foggies are up to and report back to the other clouds who float higher up. The Foggies need as much low cloud as possible to darken the world and they want us to float down to their level and join in. But we won't. They must extinguish the lights of the North Star to fully achieve their dastardly master plan. Even Santa Paws won't know which way to go if he can't see the North Star. Grumpy as I am, I want Christmas to happen as much as you do because every year, Santa Paws sprinkles some Christmas cheer on me when he flies past."

"Phew! I am very pleased to hear that. But you still let them take my Wim-Wim. And my toast is in it," said Badger.

"I had to, otherwise they would have rumbled me and known I wasn't on their side. As the Nimbus Ambassador, I had two fluffy wisps crossed behind my back which allowed me to fib when I signed us up to their scheme. Now you want to know where they've taken your Wim-Wim with its precious cargo, don't you?"

"I do indeed, otherwise Christmas can't happen, I won't get any of my stashed toast, and the world will be cast into darkness. Nippy, we are only hours away from Christmas Day," said Badger urgently.

"The North Star is safe for now. But it's being held captive in the darkest, most depressing place ever – the Mopery. There's no light there, barely any air, nothing ever happens, everything is stagnant. The atmosphere will suffocate the star."

"The Mopery? The woeful place that squashes all va-va-vooms?" squealed Ella. Nippy nodded.

"But how do we get there?" asked Badger urgently.

"You need a guide to take you there. Only the blue light energy of an inhabitant of Sirius, the Dog Star, can penetrate the Mopery. Why don't you visit the Enchanted Forest and see who you might meet?" winked Nippy, "Have you got your password?"

"Seriously Nippy, with everything that's at stake, do you still need to play the Big Bad Gatekeeper to the Enchanted Forest? Do I really need the password this time?"

"I'm afraid so, Badger, especially when you have an unannounced guest with you."

Ella stepped forward and bent her beak down to face Nippy upside down. "I'm Gabriella, the Snow Goose, but my friends call me Ella. I'm the one who has been entrusted with the mission of delivering the star back to its pole position."

Badger was scratching his head and thinking of the possible password. "Jingle Bells?"

Suddenly a rope ladder unfurled from Nippy's mists. Badger wagged his tail and made his way down with Ella perched on his head.

"Be careful, Badger," warned Nippy. "The Sparkle Bandits mean business. They've been waiting a long time for this opportunity to avenge the Big and Wee Folk for all their moans and groans about the weather."

Chapter Five

When Badger stepped off the final rung of the ladder, he felt soft, fresh snow underpaw. He looked around to see a large crowd wearing hats and scarves assembled in front of him.

"Uh-oh, they must have known we were coming," Badger groaned.

"Don't be silly," honked Ella. "Can't you see they are snowmen?"

"Oh yes, of course. That carrot looks tasty," drooled Badger.

"Don't touch that. It's his nose. What's that over there?" asked Ella.

"It's a signpost," said Badger hopefully.

On the left it said *GETTING WARMER*, and on the right, it pointed to *GETTING COLDER*. On top of the signpost there was a giant Christmas cracker.

"How exciting!" shrieked Ella, "Pleeeeeeeeeeeeeeeeeeeeeaase, can we pull it now?"

"Of course," said Badger, wondering if there was any possibility of some toast inside.

Ella flew up to catch one end of the cracker in her beak and brought the other end down to Badger's paws.

"One, two, three, pull!" yelled Badger.

With a yank, a *snap* and a *pop*, the cracker burst open hurling Badger and Ella backwards in the snow.

"I won, I won," shrieked Ella excitedly, poking her beak inside. She pulled out two paper hats, a small red magnet and a piece of paper.

"Put your hat on, Badger, and I'll read out the joke." Ella cleared her throat and read:

"Because of where you need to go,
Where everything is bleak,
You must take the rules you know
And reverse-play Hide and Seek.

The colder you get,
The warmer you are.
Where icicles hang,
You are not far."

Ella shrugged her wings and said, "That's not even funny. That's a rubbish joke."

"That's because it's not a joke, Ella. It's a riddle and it's giving us a clue about which way to go."

"Ah, so normally in *Hide and Seek*, if you're *getting warmer*, it means you're getting nearer to whoever is hiding," said Ella.

"Correct, except I think the riddle is telling us to follow the GETTING COLDER path," said Badger.

"Are you absolutely sure?" asked Ella.

"Yes, but you're the one with the inbuilt navigation system."

"Yes, but you're the one who is supposed to be magical. Can't you look in your snow globe?"

"Of course, I forgot about that," he winked. He shook the globe until an image settled of an ice cream cone.

"That's clear. We should take the GETTING COLDER path," smiled Badger.

"Not necessarily," honked Ella, "An ice cream cone could mean the summer, so we should take the *GETTING WARMER* path instead."

Badger sighed and set off on the right-hand path. He tucked the little magnet into his neckerchief. Both he and Ella were still wearing their Christmas party hats.

"Brrrrr," shivered Badger. "It's definitely getting much colder." Ella brushed past a row of hanging icicles which tinkled out a merry tune. They continued on in the silence until they spotted something that looked like a statue up ahead. As they drew closer, they saw it was a magnificent ice sculpture. On it there was a big notice stating *DO NOT TOUCH*. Badger leaned forward and prodded it with his paw. Suddenly cracks started to appear in the figure.

"Ooops," said Badger looking back at Ella in apology. "It's like a *WET PAINT* sign. I just can't resist checking to see if the paint is still wet."

Ella flapped her wings crossly.

The sculpture cracked some more and then shards of ice sprung off.

Badger and Ella jolted backwards apprehensively.

They watched wide-eyed as the sculpture shattered completely. Out of the ice splinters, a majestic sheepdog with glittering blue eyes emerged. Its black fur was speckled with patches of white and flecks of indigo. The creature shook itself, walked over to Badger and held out its paw.

"Hello, Badger. I'm Virginia Woof, at your service. You can call me *Jin*. I'm so glad you worked out my riddle. I've been expecting you."

Badger was speechless and a little overawed at her intense, blue gaze. He was sure he'd heard of Virginia Woof before. Even unflappable Ella was dumbstruck.

"So, are you sure that

you are willing to risk your feel-good factor by visiting the misery of the Mopery?" asked Jin.

Badger and Ella nodded vigorously. Their cheery festive hats fell off.

"Yes, we must. We have to rescue the North Star to save Christmas and stop the darkness."

"If you really are sure then your goodness will shield you from the worst. I've just landed from Sirius, the Dog Star. You see, the North Star's ancient name means 'dog's tail', that's why you were invited on this mission, Badger, and also why I can help," said the sheepdog.

The Mystical Mutt gulped as he realised the enormity of the mission.

"Follow me to the Revolving Igloo and we'll hook up your snow globe to its internal navigation system," beckoned Jin.

Badger's ears pricked up. "How do you know about my snow globe?"

"Captain Bravebark sent me, so I have a nose for what needs to be known," smiled Jin, tapping her nose with her paw.

At the Mopery, the star was dazzling the darkness with spangles of luminosity.

The Bleak Brothers were distressed – there was too much glow for their gloom. They had to find a way to stifle the sparkle, as they were stuck at the very core of the radiance. More junior clouds bore less of the brunt and had thickly shrouded the star from Earth.

Humdrum and Dumdrum tried raining on it without much success. The water droplets just reflected back and magnified the brightness bouncing around the Mopery.

They tried blowing on it with even worse results. The star swayed and swung like a giant glitter ball dispersing shards of light into every dismal nook and dreary cranny.

"I know," piped up Humdrum, "We need to black it out totally."

"Agreed, but how exactly do we do that then?" said Dumdrum.

"Soot, of course," said Humdrum smugly. "Let's send a Cloud Crew to suck up a trillion tonnes of soot from a zillion Christmas chimneys."

"Good plan, but then what?" asked Dumdrum

"Then we blast the star with soot and cover it completely."

"Brilliant plan," gasped Dumdrum. "But what do we do right now to stop the glare?"

"We use sunglasses, my friend."

"Excellent idea," said Dumdrum. "Where do we get those then?"

"You drift down to *The Eye in the Sky's* sunshade shop and pick up as many pairs as possible. I'll keep watch here. Quick, before it closes," ordered Humdrum.

Dumdrum floated off and soon came back with a bumper batch of sunglasses.

But when the Cloud Crew returned to the Mopery full of soot, they were sneezing and coughing. Everything, except the North Star, was covered in a thick, black smirr.

Humdrum and Dumdrum sighed and sank even deeper into their dourness.

Badger, Ella and Jin arrived at the Revolving Igloo and waited until the doorway gap spun around. Jin strode confidently inside, while Badger and Ella stepped gingerly through the opening.

Inside was a massive rotating globe. It was Earth, and its axis at the North Pole was wobbling. A map of the Mopery took central position on the main wall. Telephones rang out across the desks and an enigmatic coding machine vibrated. A mass of coloured Post-it notes were stuck to various whiteboards around the ice blocks. Cameras whirred, computers clicked and hubs buzzed.

Badger flinched. This was a nerve centre, and he felt a bit nervous.

He suddenly remembered where he'd heard Jin's name before. She'd been awarded the Order of the Bark for canine gallantry and bravery several years running. He'd read about her in *Paws of the World* and seen her photograph.

"Here's the plan to rescue the North Star," said Jin briskly. "Once we have it, we need to take it temporarily to the Star Sanctuary for safe keeping. Badger, you've been there often, I think."

Badger looked at her blankly. He didn't think he'd ever been to the Star Sanctuary. Jin shook her head and walked over to the rotating globe. It was surrounded by a circular control panel pulsating with coloured light pads. "Badger, place your snow globe on the blue pad here," Jin said. As soon as the Mystical Mutt set the snow globe on the pad, a blast of blue light shot through it and a musical note boomed out. Badger and Ella looked around wide-eyed.

"Wow!" jumped Badger and leaned on a red light pad next to a blue one. Another musical note rang out. Ella honked in delight, flew up onto the control panel and hopped from pad to pad. With Badger's pounding paws and Ella's welly boots, they tried to play the tune of *Jingle Bells*.

Jin barked loudly and said: "Have you both quite finished? This is a serious mission." Badger and Ella stopped immediately. Jin pointed to Badger's snow globe. They peered at the image that was slowly emerging.

"The information has now been passed from your snow globe to the igloo's radar. It can guide us to the Star Sanctuary, in case Nippy Nimbus can't help us."

"Why wouldn't Nippy be able to help us?" asked Badger.

"Because he's a cloud, after all, and right now clouds are our enemy," continued Jin. "Ella, you're the assigned Custodian of the Star and the star therefore trusts you to carry its sparkle to safety. Badger, you'll need to dust off some of your spells as we will need some powerful magic to protect us. I can penetrate the Mopery, so I hope we're all ready. Time is running out for us to save Christmas. I, as you can see, am Commander-in-Chief. Follow my lead and we won't go wrong."

"But you've not got a lead for us to follow," Ella pointed out.

"Not *that* kind of lead," said Jin rolling her eyes, "but I can assure you that I have the whole support of my very own Dog Star, Sirius, behind us. Plus, I have my cloud-busting technology." She showed them a strange-looking device strapped to her fore-leg. Badger and Ella nodded impressively at the metallic funnel-shaped contraption.

Badger scratched his head and looked at Jin doubtfully.

"Star Sanctuary?" he asked. "Are you sure I've been there before?"

"Of course, Badger. It's at the Crystal Cave, here in the Enchanted Forest. But first we must get to the Mopery and rescue the star. With every snowflake that falls, the Christmas countdown is getting closer."

"Terrific!" muttered Badger picking up his snow globe. "Lead the way then, Jin."

"There's only one way to go. Are you up for the slide down the Bobsleigh Burrow?"

Ella and Badger swallowed and nodded.

Chapter Six

Jin waved at the igloo wall.

"Why are you waving at ice?" asked Badger, baffled.

"It's a high-security paw-recognition beam," smiled Jin, as blocks of ice at the back of the igloo criss-crossed then slid apart to reveal a chamber gleaming with ice-blue light. A sleek bobsleigh bedecked with bells awaited them.

"Come on, jump aboard! And hold on tight," commanded Jin.

Ella and Badger stepped inside the chamber and climbed aboard the sleigh. Jin shoved the sleigh from behind and it started to move. As the aerodynamic shell gathered speed, Jin leapt quickly onto the seat behind Badger. The sleigh tipped forward and whizzed into a long downhill burrow.

"Woaaaaaaaaaaaaaaaaah!" screeched Ella as they hurtled at top speed past the curved walls of ice, twisting and turning down the tunnel. Badger clung on tightly. All he could see were wings and welly boots as Ella held onto him with all her might. At last, the sleigh seemed to tilt upwards. It slowed

down and swooshed sharply to a
halt. The bells jingled.

"We've arrived," said Jin
jumping out. Badger stepped
off dizzily and Ella wobbled off
behind him.

"Wow!" sighed Ella,
unruffling her wings. "That
was both thrilling and
terrifying. Where are we now?"

"I don't want to worry
anyone, but look at that," Badger
squirmed, pointing to a large
sign above two steel doors.
The sign read *Panic Station*.

"Whatever you do, don't
panic," said Jin calmly. She
winked at Badger and pressed a
button to the side of the doors.

"I never panic," gulped
Badger, starting to panic.

Badger and Ella looked at each
other then looked up and up
... and up at a sky-scraping
lift shaft.

PANIC STATION

The doors pinged open.

Badger and Ella followed Jin into a large shiny lift. Each mirrored wall was lined with buttons from floor to ceiling. Each button bore a floor number and a name. Badger scanned the buttons trying to find *The Mopery* floor.

"This is *Panic Station*," announced an automated voice. "You are currently at floor number 3. Only 5,040 more floors until you reach your destination. Please stand clear of the closing doors."

"Floor 3,678, *Pie in the Sky*? Oh, can we stop there? I'm suddenly very hungry," drooled Badger. "My toast supply is in the Wim-Wim." Jin nudged Badger's paw away from the button just in time.

"We came here to visit one place, and one place only, Badger. Now, focus on our mission," she scolded.

Jin reached up with her paw and pressed the highest button. It lit up with a sign saying *The Mopery*. The doors snapped shut and the voice said, "Going up." They watched as a neon arrow above the door moved up through the floor numbers and names. They passed: *110, Pillar to Post; 202, Rock and a Hard Place; 890, Coast to Coast; 4,853, The Shambles; 4,854, The Eye in the Sky;* and *4,899, Sixes and Sevens.*

Then suddenly, *ding!* The lift lurched, tilted and shook from side to side. A siren rang out and a red light flashed. *Ding!* "Do not be alarmed. We are experiencing some technical difficulties. Please exit when doors open," said the robotic voice. The doors flew open and threw them all out. Giant number sixes and number sevens scurried about smirking.

"Oh no!" said Badger. "We're at Sixes and Sevens. We need to scarper fast or we'll be stuck here, lost forever." Enormous number sixes and sevens loomed over them.

"Yikes!" yelled Jin, "Our days are numbered. Quick, get back in the lift before we get digitised."

They raced back in and the doors slammed shut just as a huge six and an even larger seven tottered towards them.

Ding! The lights on the buttons flashed again before they whooshed up to floor 5,002. It juddered to a stop then plummeted down to floor number 26. *Ding*! "*Boxing Day*," said the lift, flinging open its doors to reveal a row of kangaroos wearing boxing gloves.

"Uh-oh. Wrong floor again," yelled Badger, frantically pressing the *Close Doors* button. But the lift tilted forward and tipped them out.

"Oh no! Duck!" shouted Jin.

"Where? I can't see any ducks," said Ella.

"Not ducks that quack," cried Badger.

"DUCK!" they screamed at Ella, pushing her to the ground. The three of them bobbed and weaved to dodge the boxing kangaroos and their random jabs. The bouncing boxers chased them back towards the lift.

"Ouch!" cried Badger as a bell rang and the doors banged shut. "That's one Boxing Day I will never forget."

Ding! The buttons flashed. "Going up. Stopping at *Fiddle Sticks*, *Fuddy-Duddy* and

Wild Goose Chase, announced the lift.

"Noooooooooooooooooooooooo, I don't like the sound of Wild Goose Chase," groaned Ella. "Can't you do a spell, Badger, and make it stop stopping?"

"And ask it to stop at the right stop instead," added Jin.

Badger scratched his head.

"Quickly please, Badger. We're getting closer to Fiddle Sticks," shouted Jin.

Badger closed his eyes and concentrated. Then he took a deep breath and said:

"Please stop stopping at Pillar to Post,
Sixes and Sevens and Coast to Coast,
Wild Goose Chase and Pie in the Sky.
Show us the place that is passing us by.
We cannot be stuck at this Sticky Wicket.
You know the level and we have the ticket.
We're getting off at The Mopery floor,
Right at the top. It's the very last door."

The lift juddered then zoomed so fast everybody's tummy lurched. It stopped sharply at floor number 5,043 and its doors sprung open. Badger's spell had actually worked. They had arrived at the Mopery. Outside the elevator, the light of the North Star, now at almost maximum wattage, dazzled them all. Clouds with huge sunglasses drifted aimlessly back and forth. Luckily, the clouds were so blinded by the light that they didn't notice the lift arriving with Badger, Ella and Jin inside.

As Jin stepped forward, Badger caught her paw,

"Hang on. You're stepping into nothing but air. Wait while I try my balloon spell,"

he said. Badger closed his eyes and uttered a
magical rhyme:

"Bring Jin balloons stuffed full of air,
A floating festival which she can wear.
Keep her safe and in suspense,
Among these clouds so glum and dense."

Multicoloured balloons
appeared out of
nowhere and attached
themselves to Jin.
    "Where are your
balloons?" Jin asked.
    "I don't need
them. I have wings,"
said Ella smugly.
    "I don't need them either.
I can fly," said Badger proudly.
    "Respect!" said Jin,
high-fiving the Mystical
Mutt. They glided out of
the elevator and into
the cheerless gloom

of the Mopery. They spotted the Wim-Wim straightaway. It was flanked by the infamous Bleak Brothers.

"I'll distract Numdrum's heavies. Ella, you grab the star and, Badger, can you do your *Razzle-Dazzle* spell again?" said Jin.

"I'll try," winced Badger.

Jin hovered around the Bleak Brothers and said, "Here cloudy-cloudy. Good clouds. Fetch!" She threw off one of her balloons and watched as Numdrum's sidekicks moved off clumsily in its direction, bumping into each other. Badger whispered the spell and focused his eyes on the precious North Star. Suddenly, it began to splinter into thousands of tiny crystals.

Badger looked down at his neckerchief and said, "'Chief, go with Ella and gather up the crystals." Ella flew around and, with her beady eyes, caught every falling crystal in her beak and popped them into the bag that 'Chief had formed. When every single crystal had been safely accounted for, Badger jumped into the Wim-Wim, followed swiftly by Jin, and took the controls. Ella perched on top and Badger plugged in his snow globe for the route to the Enchanted Forest and the Crystal Cave within. The Wim-Wim tilted forwards and shot off.

At last, Badger was reunited with his stash of toast.

But the sky had darkened without the brilliant light of the North Star. The Sparkle Bandits threw off their sunglasses and set out in pursuit.

Chapter Seven

From her vantage point on top of the Wim-Wim, Ella was first to see the heavy clouds rolling in.

"We've got company, everyone," she shouted, flapping her wings at the Wim-Wim's portholes.

"We can out-fly them," yelled Badger. "There's no wind in the Mopery, and the Foggies are too heavy with rain to move faster than my Wim-Wim."

Ella glanced nervously behind her. The clouds were managing to keep pace.

"There's Nippy up ahead," shouted Badger. "We're almost there. It's half past ten. We've nearly done it. We've saved the North Star, and Christmas."

Suddenly, Jin pointed her funnel-shaped contraption at the Foggies and fired a blast of steam.

"What's that?" asked Badger.

"It's a trick I learned from a Costa-Rican Bush Dog. It fills the clouds with even more rain which slows them down. It's the cloud-busting machine I showed you earlier," said Jin proudly.

Immediately, the nearest clouds fell back and Badger thrust forward towards his faithful friend, Nippy Nimbus.

Badger landed the Wim-Wim and pleaded, "This is an emergency, Nippy. We have no time for passwords."

"Then be on your way, and good luck," said Nippy kindly. "Remember always to trust me though, Badger, even if it seems that I have betrayed you. And always put your mission first, as it is for the greater good."

Badger looked confused and slid the Wim-Wim through the gap in Nippy to land swiftly in the Enchanted Forest.

Meanwhile Nippy Nimbus could see Numdrum, the Bleak Brothers and the rest of the Foggies wafting ominously closer.

"Follow me," said Jin. "We need to get to the Crystal Cave and shelter the star in the Star Sanctuary."

Badger and Ella let Jin lead the way along the frosty path towards the glinting opening. Soon, they arrived, and Jin beckoned them inside towards a gleaming chamber at the very back of the cave.

"Here is our Star Sanctuary. It's time to secure our star," said Jin, pointing her paw at Badger's neckerchief hanging from Ella's beak.

Ella laid the precious parcel carrying the North Star crystals on the cave floor.

"Be as still as you can everyone," whispered Jin. Her blue eyes glowed.

Swirls of light swept around the neckerchief as a spiral galaxy of crystal clusters flared throughout the cave. One by one, each sparkle embedded itself within the walls. The cave glistened. Badger's neckerchief, now empty, returned to his neck. He patted it fondly.

"The North Star is safe for now," Jin nodded. "Let's return and find out how far the Foggies have got."

"But do we have to?" asked Badger. "We've saved the star. Surely our job is done?"

"We may have rescued the star for now," said Ella, "but Christmas still can't happen unless we return the star to its pole position before midnight."

"It's already quarter past eleven, we must defeat the Sparkle Bandits once and for all," said Jin bravely.

"Agreed," said Badger firmly. "Let's go back."

Back at Nippy Nimbus, the grumpy cloud was surrounded by Numdrum, the Bleak Brothers and a sunken soufflé of rain clouds.

"You have betrayed us, your own kind, Nippy!" hissed Numdrum, the Director of Doom.

"You're not my kind. You're committing a crime against clouds," puffed Nippy.

"You want to darken the world and destroy Christmas. If you succeed, clouds like me will cease to exist because we will have sunk to your level and the sun will never shine again."

"Do I look like I care? You will be punished, but not before you grant us access to where those idiots have taken the North Star. *Then,* we'll see just how much your beloved Badger is willing to fight for you."

"No, never," said Nippy.

"Have it your own way," said Numdrum. "But if you won't let us through, remember we are heavier than you, and there are many more of us, so we can crush you. Our vapour will overcome you, we will absorb you, and you, Nippy Nimbus, will expire.

"You can try," trembled Nippy bravely, "but I will always be higher than you."

"Not for long," Numdrum motioned to Humdrum and Dumdrum to begin squashing Nippy.

"Ouch!" squealed Nippy, feeling the depressing darkness start to seep into his fluffiness. "Okay, I surrender, there's the gap. Go on then. Bluster through." Nippy cried.

Leaving Nippy intact and unsquished, the Director of Doom slid through the opening, followed by the Bleak Brothers and the rest of the Foggies. They descended into the sky above the Enchanted Forest. There, they hovered threateningly, waiting for their prey.

Chapter Eight

Badger and the others sensed the skies darken and the air change.

"They're here," whispered Badger. "Nippy must have let them through. I can't believe it. I thought Nippy was my friend ... sort of."

"He must have had good reason to allow them access to this sacred place, Badger," said Jin wisely. "Remember Nippy's last words to you – to trust him, even if it seems he has betrayed you?"

"I've got an idea," said Ella, "With the star safe for now, let's disguise ourselves as Christmas trees. I've made a tree before. It's easy."

"Good plan," said Badger, wishing he had thought of it himself. "Then we can sidle slowly to the Wim-Wim and make a getaway. They'll never know it's us," he added.

"And the frost will give us Christmas sparkles," said Ella excitedly.

Jin sped off to find some evergreen laurel, pieces of privet, twigs and bristly fir for their tree disguises. Soon, three peculiar Christmas trees appeared side by side in the Enchanted Forest.

"Ella and Jin, are you ready?" asked Badger.

"Yes!" replied the trees.

"Right, after three and slowly does it. One, two, three and ... shuffle," ordered Badger. The wonky trees tottered along then stopped. The trees shuffled again and wobbled.

"This is tooooooooooooo much fun," Ella squealed.

"Ssshhhh," scolded Jin. "Focus!"

"I can't see where I'm going," giggled Badger.

In the distance, the Director of Doom heard the chattering and tumbled further into the forest. He scanned the ground below for any sign of movement. Suddenly, he spotted something shift slightly in his sights.

"What is it, boss?" asked the Bleak Brothers.

"Possibly the strangest moving Christmas trees I've ever seen," wheezed Numdrum.

"Where?" asked the daft duo.

"Over there," Numdrum shouted to the Bleak Brothers, nodding towards the tip-toeing trees. "Blow a gale now!" Humdrum and Dumdrum hung over the spot and blew hard. All the makeshift leaves and greenery scattered to reveal the three friends sprackled on the floor. Badger looked up to see Numdrum, Humdrum and Dumdrum with their squadron of Sparkle Bandits cackling above.

"Aha," grimaced the Mystical Mutt. "I see you made it then."

"Thanks to help from your friend Nippy Nimbus, we gained access through the hidden gap," sneered Numdrum.

Badger frowned.

"So, it's as simple as this," spat Numdrum: "give us back the North Star or

we will vapourise Nippy Nimbus and you
will never see him again."

Badger gulped.

This was one decision he was not happy
making. Should he forsake his friend or save
Christmas?

Chapter Nine

Badger looked uneasily from Ella to Jin.

"Only you can make this choice, Badger," said Ella.

"Nippy said to put your mission first for the greater good," Jin reminded him.

Badger touched his trusted neckerchief anxiously.

"Well, what's it to be? The clock's ticking. The Christmas countdown is almost finished. It's make-your-mind-up time," taunted Numdrum.

Badger looked at 'Chief again. It was sparkling and aglow with light. He knew his answer.

"Do what you want with Nippy. He's always so grumpy. He's no friend of mine," whispered Badger sadly.

"That's a big mistake, Badger. We'll destroy Nippy anyway, but we still want that star. So give it back now," boomed Numdrum.

"You'll have to find it first," said Badger.

"You *will* show us, or we'll flood your precious forest and everything in it will drown," threatened Numdrum.

"Not so fast," shouted Jin as her piercing eyes pointed directly at the Director of Doom. Two magnificent laser beams shot forth from each eye and immediately blinded Numdrum, the Bleak Brothers and all the Foggies. They scattered clumsily across the sky.

"Wow, Jin! Where did you learn to do that?" said Badger in amazement.

"I'm from the Dog Star, Sirius. We have these skills built in. And I did mention that we have the entire support of the planet," replied Jin, puffing out her chest. "After all, everyone loves Christmas! But the effects of the lasers won't last long, so over to you, Badger, for the next step. How do we get rid of them for good?"

and the Sparkle Bandits

Badger scratched his head and said, "I do have a rough plan, but I'll need your expertise to identify the magnetic ley lines of the forest. Then I might be able to conjure up the Rain Drain spell."

"I like it already," said Jin. "I'll map out the ley lines and then I can figure out the grid coordinates, if that helps."

Ella honked her approval. Jin rushed off around the forest and Badger began working on the spell.

But first, he thought, *we will need a large umbrella*.

He looked down at his neckerchief and muttered a spell.

"'*Chief, chief, please become an enormous brolly,*

Big enough to shield Snow Goose and Collie."
The neckerchief unfurled from Badger's neck and shapeshifted into a huge nylon canopy.

"Ella, look, get under my umbrella," grinned Badger.

"Golly, that's impressive, Badger," said Ella waddling over to the giant brolly.

"'Chief can do almost anything when I ask nicely. Now, how quickly can you build a nest lined with leaves?"

"Super-fast. It's a speciality of mine," she winked.

Badger gathered the ingredients for his Rain Drain spell.

Dandelion, hawthorn and juniper green,
Juice of a lemon and sap of a dream,
Mallow and basil with Old Father Thyme,
All blended up with the zest of a lime.

Jin returned with her magnetic ley-line coordinates and Ella presented her robustly built nest. Badger placed everything into it, adding the red magnet he'd kept from the Christmas cracker. *I knew that would come in handy,* he thought, *especially to attract the electromagnetic rain drain.*

He got ready to recite the all important spell. Flickers of light danced above his head as he concentrated.

But the Foggies were no longer dazzled by the laser beams and had clustered around Badger's umbrella, where Ella and Jin huddled expectantly.

"Nice try, Badger, but we can see you again. Now, where were we? Ah yes, we were about to unleash a deluge of showers upon you and your forest." warned the Director of Doom. "I don't think your brolly

will save you from what we've got. We're fully laden and ready to pour."

As Numdrum commanded the Foggies to flood the forest, Badger held his paws high and charged the nest before him with his magic.

"With lines of the ley, and the magnetic key,
Let all that is nesting answer our plea.
When the clouds drop their rain,
And the snow turns to mush,
Spawn us a drain,
To take it, and flush

93

Down the big plughole.
Send it into a spin,
Then suck up the clouds,
And take them all in."

Relentless rain battered down from the Foggies and at the same time, a giant drain appeared in the ground before them, alongside an enormous bath plug.

The rain drained immediately down the plughole and created a vacuum which sucked every rain droplet from the ground and the air around. Then one by one, each of the Foggies was swallowed up and swept down the plughole too.

Jin and Badger heaved the bath plug over the top of the drain and breathed out in relief.

Everything was quiet. The rain had stopped and the sky had brightened.

"Phew!" said Badger. "Well, that's got rid of them. Now, let's get the star and go and see if Nippy is still in one piece."

When they reached the Crystal Cave, Ella collected the thousands of crystals and placed them again inside Badger's neckerchief. With the star package safely in Ella's beak, they boarded the Wim-Wim and set off to see Nippy.

But as they took off happily, one of the Sparkle Bandits remained in the Enchanted Forest. The Director of Doom had escaped the rain drain and was watching everything.

There were only fifteen minutes until Christmas Day.

Chapter Ten

Badger steered the Wim-Wim to twenty past the Southern Fogbow where Nippy usually hung about, but the grumpy cloud was nowhere to be seen.

"Oh no!" cried Badger. "Numdrum meant what he said. He's vaporised Nippy."

"Maybe Nippy has met another cloud and floated off on the Jet Stream?" offered Jin hopefully.

"Perhaps he's gone to Cloud Cuckoo Land for the holidays?" honked Ella.

Badger sighed and shook his head.

"I don't think so," he replied sadly. "There's not another cloud in the sky that could put up with his grumpiness. I know I disowned him to Numdrum as my friend, but I didn't mean it. Nippy might be the most bad-tempered cloud in the world, but he actually *was* my friend. He's helped me out so many times."

Ella wrapped her wings around him. Jin stood tall and said, "I know you're worried, Badger, but we've got a mission to complete and time is against us. Nippy would want you to carry on with your task. Now, come on, let's get back on course. I've got to get back to Sirius for Christmas Day, and there's only twelve minutes left."

"Of course," agreed Badger shaking himself.

He set the Wim-Wim's satnav for the North Pole and the flying machine climbed higher and higher in the dark cloudless sky, the only sound its steady hum as it travelled through the stars.

Suddenly the Wim-Wim jolted as a rumble pierced the silence.

"Oh," said Badger, "we must have hit a bit of turbulence again."

"I don't think so," shouted Ella. "Look outside."

They peered out and came face to face with the Director of Doom.

"You don't get rid of me that easily," shouted Numdrum. "Now, hand over the star."

"We haven't got it. We're on our way home," fibbed Badger.

"So why are you en route to the North Pole?" asked Numdrum.

"Because it's nearly Christmas and that's where the magic happens," suggested Ella innocently.

"Just hand it over. You can't fool me," roared Numdrum.

"But there's only you. Where are the rest of the Foggies and your silly sidekicks, the Bleak Brothers? Didn't they disappear down the plughole? You're in a bit of a fankle, out here on your own," replied Badger.

"And now that you've made Nippy dissolve, you can't call in the higher clouds for help, because we know they never actually signed up to this for real," added Ella.

The Director of Doom quivered.

"Look," said Badger attempting to sway Numdrum, "why don't you halt your mission to turn the world dark? We're only ten minutes away from Christmas Day. Why don't you just give it up and let Christmas happen?"

"Because I'd be letting my fellow clouds down," said Numdrum.

"Why not just lay low and let us carry on?" asked Jin.

"I can't. I'd go down in cloud history as the most rubbish cloud ever," he frowned.

Suddenly, Badger perked up and said: "But what if you were remembered in cloud history as having helped to save Christmas?"

"What utter twaddle!" roared Numdrum. "I've done everything I can to destroy

Christmas! I'm not changing tack now. I think it's time to unleash my Vomit Comet." He puffed up his billowing cloud cheeks and blew with all his might.

The Wim-Wim vibrated violently with the force. Numdrum blew another blast and the Wim-Wim spun around, throwing its occupants flat against its frame, their cheeks chattering and their tummies heaving.

"Jin," yelled Badger, "can you use your laser beam eyes again to stop this? The Wim-Wim can't take much more of this intense G-force, and we only have eight minutes before Christmas."

Jin tried, but nothing happened. The Wim-Wim just kept jiggling. "It's too wobbly," she cried. "My laser beams are squiggling. I can't focus."

"This calls for an emergency spell then," shouted Badger. "Ella, can you reach the grasses and grains I brought for your dinner, and, much as it hurts me, a piece of toast? 'Chief," he continued, looking down at his trusty neckerchief, "can you grab the lightning conductor from up above on the Wim-Wim's brolly?"

The neckerchief unravelled from Badger's neck and flew upwards. Ella rushed forward with her ingredients.

Numdrum was still blowing hard and fast. The Wim-Wim was being battered even more. 'Chief returned with the lightning conductor and Badger uttered his crucial spell to save his beloved travelling machine and all of its passengers.

*"Strike of lightning, make this mix
Into quickly sticky, gooey fix;
A Christmas pudding like no other,
To cover Numdrum in a smother."*

The lightning conductor sizzled and sparked then *BOOM!* A giant Christmas pudding burst out of nowhere and splattered everything and everyone in its path. Then it shot out of the Wim-Wim and plastered itself over Numdrum, covering the cloud in a syrupy gloop. The Wim-Wim stopped spinning. Badger licked his fur. Ella pecked the pudding from her pink welly boots. Jin nuzzled her own sweet-tasting coat.

"Yum! That's my most tasty spell yet." Badger slurped happily.

They looked out at Numdrum who was hanging heavily in mid-air seeping sticky goo.

"Ha, ha," chuckled Badger. "Numdrum's raining Christmas pudding."

Badger, Ella and Jin burst out laughing.

"What happened?" glowered Numdrum. "What is this stuff?"

"Merry Christmas! You look good enough to eat," giggled Badger.

Ella and Jin continued to chuckle.

"What's so funny?" asked the Director of Doom.

"You," pointed Ella sniggering. "You look like a right pudding."

"I feel somewhat bamboozled," said Numdrum stifling a chortle.

"Did you just laugh there?" asked Jin in amazement.

"No, no, no, noooo ... ho, no ... ho, no ... ho ho ho!" protested the Director of Doom.

"Are you possibly feeling just a teensy-weensy bit jolly?" smiled Badger.

"Surely not! I *am* the Director of Doom, after all. Is this what Christmas cheer feels like?"

"Why not let me tickle your tummy and we can find out," said Badger leaning out of the Wim-Wim.

"All I need is a few wisps from that fluffy underbelly – the one I know you have but never show. I can make you more famous for doing good than you could ever be for doing bad."

106

"Nonsense. I don't believe you," bellowed the cloud.

"It's true. I can do it. They don't call me the Mystical Mutt for nothing. You need to trust me," said Badger.

"Why should I trust you when you have flushed most of my kind down a giant plughole?" said Numdrum.

"It's your choice. But doesn't happy feel much better than gloomy?"

Numdrum shrugged and oozed more Christmas pudding.

"Just one more question or I'll send you off to Sticky Wicket: What did you do to Nippy Nimbus?" continued Badger.

"Nothing," said Numdrum. "In the end, we never touched him. He let us through after all. He should be called *Wimpy* Nimbus."

"Oh," said Badger, relieved but puzzled. "Right, drop any leftover pudding and be on your way. We need to deliver a star. We'll deal with you later!"

Numdrum skulked off.

At five minutes to Christmas Day, the Big Folk and Wee Folk in Honolulu experienced a short and sudden Christmas pudding shower even though the weather forecast was for clear skies.

Chapter Eleven

A few minutes later, Badger, Ella and Jin watched with awe as the Wim-Wim approached the glacial majesty of the North Pole.

"I need to call in some help for landing now, Badger," said Jin gravely.

"But we can see it. We can see exactly where the star needs to go. There's a blue light glowing on the snow globe sat nav. *You have arrived at your destination*, it says," said Badger.

"It's not quite as simple as that," replied Jin. "The star must reconfigure itself from the thousands of crystals in your neckerchief. There's a celestial runway ahead of us that's invisible to your snow globe's sat nav. We need the help of a

Blessing of Unicorns. They will be our air-traffic control."

"But you're from Sirius! Why do we need more than you?" asked Ella.

"I'd be the most magical dog ever if I could handle this landing on my own," said Jin modestly. She pointed her laser eyes ahead, "Badger, we need to fly due north through that line of stars there."

Badger nodded and steered the Wim-Wim through the midnight sky towards the twinkling corridor. Shooting stars heralded their entrance to the runway. As they passed each star, Jin bowed her head towards the centre of each. A blast of light shot forth and each star was transformed into a spectacular white unicorn.

Badger and Ella watched open-mouthed and Jin smiled knowingly. The unicorns herded together and guided the Wim-Wim to a precise spot in the sky, blessing the Wim-Wim's course to the celestial runway as it passed. They landed with only one minute to go until Christmas Day.

"Welcome to Ursa Minor," smiled Jin. "Many think this constellation is bear-like, but in times past, it was seen as a dog. That's why Captain Bravebark knew it had to be you, Badger, and me, from the Dog Star, Sirius, on Ella's mission. Over to you now, Ella. Be quick!"

Ella stepped off the Wim-Wim with her precious cargo wrapped in Badger's neckerchief and spread her wings. The thirty-second Christmas countdown had begun. The Blessing of Unicorns encircled her. She tapped the parcel three times with her beak. At once, thousands of crystals burst out in all their glory, shining, swirling and cascading with grandeur as they joined together again and reshaped into the North Star.

A choir of angels began to sing, bells jingled and a mischief of elves appeared from nowhere to dance around the star. Badger, Ella and Jin watched wide-eyed as the Blessing of Unicorns bowed their heads and turned back into stars.

Something else caught Badger's eye. There, smiling as he had never before, and lit up beautifully by the North Star, was his old pal, Nippy Nimbus.

"What took you so long?" asked Nippy. "I knew you'd do it, so I thought I'd get here first. But you did cut it a bit fine!"

Badger's tail wagged speedily as he bounced happily around the Wim-Wim.

A sleigh approached from behind and on it, a red-suited, white-bearded husky saluted Badger and his friends. A reindeer stuck its very red nose inside the Wim-Wim and snorted a greeting to Jin.

"Is that who I think it is?" honked Ella.

"Santa Paws himself," grinned Jin.

"We've done it," yelled Badger, high-fiving Jin and Ella. "Christmas is back on track. We've saved the most magical day of all."

"Not quite yet," said Numdrum looming before them again.

"Remember me? Remember your promise?"

Everyone groaned.

Chapter Twelve

"Of course," said Badger, "I always remember my promises. My vow to you, in return for helping us save Christmas, is to make you more famous for doing good deeds than infamous for doing dastardly deeds, correct?"

Numdrum nodded

Jin and Ella watched expectantly.

"Hover right there, Numdrum, and I will perform my festive *Fluff and Stuff* spell on you," ordered Badger, feeling much more confident now that Christmas had been saved.

The Director of Doom floated perfectly still as Badger tickled his underbelly again, plucked five white wisps and uttered the spell.

"Of Fluffy puffy cotton wool
Make Numdrum be forever full.
Not Dumper of Gloom but Bringer of Glee
These silky wisps will always be
For Santa Paws, his cuffs and beard
Sprinkled with sparkle, forever cheered"

"What happens now?" asked Numdrum.

"As it's now the exact moment between Christmas Eve and Christmas Day, the magic will be even more powerful. Across the land *whenever* and *wherever* you see Wee Folks' homemade Christmas cards with cotton wool, or you spot Santa Paws and his fluffy white beard, think of yourself, because that's where you will be. You will be a special part of Christmas, Numdrum, and I hereby rename you Director of Trimmings" said Badger triumphantly.

"The Foggies and I may have failed to turn the world dark by stealing the North Star, and trying to stop Christmas, but this actually feels better. Badger, thank you, you've made me feel useful and happy. I'll

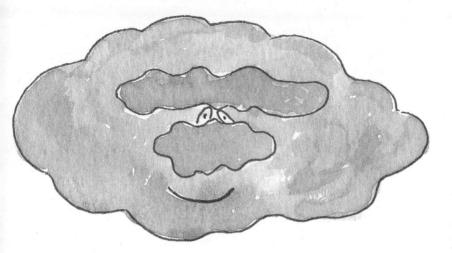

be honoured among all my kind. Uh-oh, I can feel that it's time to leave now," uttered Numdrum as he dissolved into thin air.

"That's thankfully the last we will see of him," said Jin.

Badger giggled and said: "Actually, we're going to be seeing more and more of him as cotton wool, but he'll be spreading joy instead of gloom."

"What do you mean?" yelled Jin.

"He's going to be popping up on Christmas cards and all sorts. Anywhere you see cotton wool, you will see Numdrum." said Badger.

"Is that a good thing?" asked Ella nervously.

"I think Numdrum is delighted with his new role, and we did hear him chuckle earlier, so I think he's a reformed cloud," said Badger warmly.

Ella tapped the Wim-Wim with her beak and beckoned them all to look behind them. There was Nippy Nimbus, beaming.

"Great! Just as we make one cloud vanish, another pops up," said Badger affectionately. "It's good to see you, Nippy, and I never thought I'd hear myself saying that. Now, why *did* you let the Sparkle Bandits into the Enchanted Forest?"

Nippy hung his head shame-faced and replied, "Because I'm more use to you if I'm the Gatekeeper to the Forest than if I'm vapour. And I knew you would outwit them. Sometimes things aren't always as they seem, but there's usually a good reason behind them."

"It looks like I'm going to have to endure your grumpiness on future forest visits," grinned Badger, "although that's twice I've seen you smile recently."

"Then that is two times too many. Full grumpiness resumes after Christmas," confirmed Nippy, stifling another smile.

"Merry Christmas then, Nippy, and thank you," said Badger.

"Good tidings to you too, Badger. Now I'll be on my way as I'm attending a marvellous Northern Lights show later."

They waved Nippy off and settled back down for the flight home.

"Why don't you all come round to mine for Christmas dinner?" suggested Badger excitedly.

"That would be lovely, Badger, but I've got to report back in at Greenland," said Ella.

Badger looked hopefully at Jin.

"Sorry, Badger," she said. "I can't either. I'm heading to the Enchanted Forest then on to the Revolving Igloo to return to Sirius."

Badger sighed and then jumped up eagerly.

"Why don't we have Christmas right here, right now, mid-flight?"

"That's a brilliant idea," said Jin. "Let's do it."

"Do what? We don't have any food or gifts!" screeched Ella.

"But we have magic," said Badger, "so anything and everything is possible. Plus, I still have my secret stash of toast."

Everyone agreed that this sounded like an extremely good plan. Badger put the Wim-Wim on autopilot and concentrated hard on his *Heart's Desire* spell. Ella honked out the tune to a Christmas carol.

"Okay, I think I've got the spell sorted. So, what would everyone like for Christmas? Ella, you go first," said Badger.

Ella didn't hesitate. "An acorn, please."

"An acorn?" said Badger. "May I ask why?"

"I'd like to plant my own oak tree back home in Greenland," replied the snow goose.

120

"Okay, I think I can do that. Jin, how about you? What would you love for Christmas?"

"You'll have to guess," said Jin coyly.

"Guess? Can you give me a clue?" replied Badger.

"I spy with my little eye ... something beginning with 'M'," said Jin.

"Meteor," shouted Badger.

"No," said Jin.

"Moon?" suggested Ella. Jin shook her head.

"Magic?" asked Badger.

"Yes and no," smiled Jin.

"At this rate, it will be next Christmas before we discover what you want, Jin."

"I can't tell you. It's a secret," said Jin mischievously.

"Well, I would like lots more hot-buttered toast" said Badger, "so let's do the spell. Close your eyes everyone."

Sparkles of light appeared around Badger's head as he uttered the magic rhyme:

"The joy of giving is second to none,
It's what makes Christmas full of fun.
So gift us all what our hearts want most,
Acorns, an 'M', please, and some toast."

A string of rainbow-coloured fairy lights whizzed around the Wim-Wim, followed by a stream of gold and silver tinsel. Ella was the first to open her eyes.

"Oops!" giggled Badger, "I don't know how that happened." He glanced over at Ella, who now had a sparkly horn stuck on top of her head, and gulped. Then he looked at his own feet and saw that he was knee-deep in breadcrumbs.

"Oh no," he cringed. "That hasn't worked at all. I am so sorry."

Ella and Jin were rolling about laughing covered in tinsel.

"Don't be sorry, Badger. It's fantastic, and we are enjoying ourselves. That's what Christmas is really about. I can use this horn for playing Hoopla, and you can give your Buddy-Bites pie a lovely crust with those

breadcrumbs when you get home," said Ella kindly.

"I actually got what I asked for," said Jin quietly and produced a shiny medal

from behind her back. Badger looked at her bashfully as she pinned it to his neckerchief.

"This is from my planet Sirius. It's the Dog Star Medal, for showing bravery during a lack of toast. Maybe I'll see you again in another century or so, Badger. Next time you look at the stars, I'll be waving to you from Sirius," said Jin.

Badger ruffled with pride and pushed the throttle forwards for the homeward journey.

"Merry Christmas everyone. It has been an epic adventure," said the Mystical Mutt as he dropped off Ella in Greenland, then Jin at the Enchanted Forest.

As he made his final descent towards his garden by the crack in the fence next to the lane, the snow globe glowed and an image of Captain Bravebark appeared.

"You did it, Badger; you saved Christmas. With a good heart, love, kindness and friendship, you stopped the world from becoming wholly dark. That's what Christmas is all about. Merry Christmas! I'll be in touch soon with your new mission."

Badger smiled. It was indeed a Badgical Magical Job Well Done. He wondered where his travels would take him next, and if he'd ever have such an exciting festive rest again.

Epilogue

Forever more, Christmases were adorned with Numdrum's cotton-wool wisps on Wee Folks' festive artwork and Santa Paws' hats. Father Christmas himself even refluffed his cuffs with some of Numdrum's essence.

The Sparkle Bandits never regrouped, although rain clouds still inhabited the skies, especially over the Northern Hemisphere. The rain clouds were happy with their necessary place in meteorology and every bit of the planet respected their worth.

In Greenland, Ella used her magical horn to plant some acorns. She was given the biggest accolade of all – the Golden Acorn Award – and her first few planted oak trees grew higher and stronger by the day. Greenland, at last, had a tiny patch of forest.

In the Enchanted Forest, the Revolving Igloo continued to revolve and was forever on alert for future Christmas catastrophes.

Whenever the sky was cloudless and clear, Badger shook his snow globe to try and see the Dog Star planet, Sirius, but all he could see was a whirly mist. However, when he looked upwards on a full moon eclipse, he was pretty sure he could see Virginia Woof waving at him.